Oliver Wendell Holmes

The Iron Gate

And other Poems

Oliver Wendell Holmes

The Iron Gate
And other Poems

ISBN/EAN: 9783744765886

Printed in Europe, USA, Canada, Australia, Japan

Cover: Foto ©Andreas Hilbeck / pixelio.de

More available books at **www.hansebooks.com**

THE IRON GATE,

AND OTHER POEMS.

BY

OLIVER WENDELL HOLMES.

BOSTON:

HOUGHTON, MIFFLIN AND COMPANY.

The Riverside Press, Cambridge.

1880.

RIVERSIDE, CAMBRIDGE:
STEREOTYPED AND PRINTED BY
H. O. HOUGHTON AND COMPANY.

CONTENTS.

THE IRON GATE,

AND OTHER POEMS.

THE IRON GATE.

READ AT THE BREAKFAST GIVEN IN HONOR OF DR. HOLMES'S
SEVENTIETH BIRTHDAY BY THE PUBLISHERS OF THE ATLAN-
TIC MONTHLY, BOSTON, DECEMBER 3, 1879.

WHERE is this patriarch you are kindly greeting ?
   Not unfamiliar to my ear his name,
Nor yet unknown to many a joyous meeting
   In days long vanished, — is he still the same,

Or changed by years, forgotten and forgetting,
   Dull-eared, dim-sighted, slow of speech and
      thought,
Still o'er the sad, degenerate present fretting,
   Where all goes wrong, and nothing as it ought ?

Old age, the graybeard ! Well, indeed, I know
      him, —
   Shrunk, tottering, bent, of aches and ills the prey;
In sermon, story, fable, picture, poem,
   Oft have I met him from my earliest day :

In my old Æsop, toiling with his bundle, —
   His load of sticks, — politely asking Death,
Who comes when called for, — would he lug or
     trundle
   His fagot for him ? — he was scant of breath.

And sad " Ecclesiastes, or the Preacher," —
   Has he not stamped the image on my soul,
In that last chapter, where the worn-out Teacher
   Sighs o'er the loosened cord, the broken bowl ?

Yes, long, indeed, I 've known him at a distance,
   And now my lifted door-latch shows him here ;
I take his shrivelled hand without resistance,
   And find him smiling as his step draws near.

What though of gilded baubles he bereaves us,
   Dear to the heart of youth, to manhood's prime ;
Think of the calm he brings, the wealth he leaves us,
   The hoarded spoils, the legacies of time !

Altars once flaming, still with incense fragrant,
   Passion's uneasy nurslings rocked asleep,
Hope's anchor faster, wild desire less vagrant,
   Life's flow less noisy, but the stream how deep !

Still as the silver cord gets worn and slender,
   Its lightened task-work tugs with lessening strain,

Hands get more helpful, voices, grown more tender,
   Soothe with their softened tones the slumberous
     brain.

Youth longs and manhood strives, but age re-
     members,
   Sits by the raked-up ashes of the past,
Spreads its thin hands above the whitening embers
   That warm its creeping life-blood till the last.

Dear to its heart is every loving token
   That comes unbidden ere its pulse grows cold,
Ere the last lingering ties of life are broken,
   Its labors ended and its story told.

Ah, while around us rosy youth rejoices,
   For us the sorrow-laden breezes sigh,
And through the chorus of its jocund voices
   Throbs the sharp note of misery's hopeless cry.

As on the gauzy wings of fancy flying
   From some far orb I track our watery sphere,
Home of the struggling, suffering, doubting, dying,
   The silvered globule seems a glistening tear.

But Nature lends her mirror of illusion
   To win from saddening scenes our age-dimmed
     eyes,

And misty day-dreams blend in sweet confusion
   The wintry landscape and the summer skies.

So when the iron portal shuts behind us,
   And life forgets us in its noise and whirl,
Visions that shunned the glaring noonday find us,
   And glimmering starlight shows the gates of pearl.

— I come not here your morning hour to sadden,
   A limping pilgrim, leaning on his staff, —
I, who have never deemed it sin to gladden
   This vale of sorrows with a wholesome laugh.

If word of mine another's gloom has brightened,
   Through my dumb lips the heaven-sent message
      came ;
If hand of mine another's task has lightened,
   It felt the guidance that it dares not claim.

But, O my gentle sisters, O my brothers,
   These thick-sown snow-flakes hint of toil's release ;
These feebler pulses bid me leave to others
   The tasks once welcome ; evening asks for peace.

Time claims his tribute ; silence now is golden ;
   Let me not vex the too long suffering lyre ;
Though to your love untiring still beholden,
   The curfew tells me — cover up the fire.

And now with grateful smile and accents cheerful,
  And warmer heart than look or word can tell,
In simplest phrase — these traitorous eyes are
    tearful —
  Thanks, Brothers, Sisters — Children — and fare-
    well !

VESTIGIA QUINQUE RETRORSUM.

AN ACADEMIC POEM.[1]

1829–1879.

WHILE fond, sad memories all around us throng
Silence were sweeter than the sweetest song;
Yet when the leaves are green and heaven is blue,
The choral tribute of the grove is due,
And when the lengthening nights have chilled the
    skies,
We fain would hear the song-bird ere he flies,
And greet with kindly welcome, even as now,
The lonely minstrel on his leafless bough.

    This is our golden year, — its golden day;
Its bridal memories soon must pass away,
Soon shall its dying music cease to ring
And every year must loose some silver string,
Till the last trembling chords no longer thrill, —
Hands all at rest and hearts forever still.

---

[1] Read at the Commencement Dinner of the Alumni of Harvard
University, June 25, 1879.

A few gray heads have joined the forming line ;
We hear our summons, — " Class of 'twenty-nine ! "
Close on the foremost, and, Alas, how few !
Are these " The Boys " our dear old Mother knew ?
Sixty brave swimmers.   Twenty — something
    more —
Have passed the stream and reached this frosty
    shore !

How near the banks these fifty years divide
When memory crosses with a single stride !
'T is the first year of stern " Old Hickory " 's rule
When our good Mother lets us out of school,
Half glad, half sorrowing, it must be confessed,
To leave her quiet lap, her bounteous breast,
Armed with our dainty, ribbon-tied degrees,
Pleased and yet pensive, exiles and A. B.'s.

Look back, O comrades, with your faded eyes,
And see the phantoms as I bid them rise.
Whose smile is that?   Its pattern Nature gave,
A sunbeam dancing in a dimpled wave ;
KIRKLAND alone such grace from Heaven could win,
His features radiant as the soul within ;
That smile would let him through Saint Peter's gate
While sad-eyed martyrs had to stand and wait.
Here flits mercurial *Farrar;* standing there,
See mild, benignant, cautious, learned *Ware,*

And sturdy, patient, faithful, honest *Hedge*,
Whose grinding logic gave our wits their edge ;
Ticknor, with honeyed voice and courtly grace ;
And *Willard* larynxed like a double bass ;
And *Channing* with his bland, superior look,
Cool as a moonbeam on a frozen brook,
While the pale student, shivering in his shoes,
Sees from his theme the turgid rhetoric ooze ;
And the born soldier, fate decreed to wreak
His martial manhood on a class in Greek,
Popkin ! How that explosive name recalls
The grand old Busby of our ancient halls !
Such faces looked from Skippon's grim platoons,
Such figures rode with Ireton's stout dragoons ;
He gave his strength to learning's gentle charms,
But every accent sounded " Shoulder arms ! "

Names, — empty names ! Save only here and there
Some white-haired listener, dozing in his chair,
Starts at the sound he often used to hear,
And upward slants his Sunday-sermon ear.

And we — our blooming manhood we regain ;
Smiling we join the long Commencement train,
One point first battled in discussion hot, —
Shall we wear gowns ? and settled: *We will not.*
How strange the scene, — that noisy boy-debate
Where embryo-speakers learn to rule the State !

This broad-browed youth,[1] sedate and sober-eyed,
Shall wear the ermined robe at Taney's side;
And he, the stripling,[2] smooth of face and slight,
Whose slender form scarce intercepts the light,
Shall rule the Bench where Parsons gave the law,
And sphynx-like sat uncouth, majestic Shaw!
Ah, many a star has shed its fatal ray
On names we loved — our brothers — where are they?
Nor these alone; our hearts in silence claim
Names not less dear, unsyllabled by fame.

How brief the space! and yet it sweeps us back
Far, far along our new-born history's track!
Five strides like this; — the Sachem rules the land;
The Indian wigwams cluster where we stand.

The second. — Lo! a scene of deadly strife —
A nation struggling into infant life;
Not yet the fatal game at Yorktown won
Where falling Empire fired its sunset gun.
LANGDON sits restless in the ancient chair, —
Harvard's grave Head, — these echoes heard his
          prayer
When from yon mansion, dear to memory still,
The banded yeomen marched for Bunker's hill.
Count on the grave triennial's thick-starred roll
What names were numbered on the lengthening
          scroll —

[1] Benjamin Robbins Curtis.   [2] George Tyler Bigelow.

Not unfamiliar in our ears they ring —
Winthrop, Hale, Eliot, Everett, Dexter, Tyng.

Another stride.   Once more at 'twenty-nine, —
GOD SAVE KING GEORGE, the Second of his line !
And is *Sir Isaac* living ?   Nay, not so, —
He followed *Flamsteed* two short years ago, —
And what about the little hump-backed man
Who   pleased   the   bygone   days   of   good   Queen
      Anne ?
What, *Pope ?* another book he 's just put out —
" The Dunciad " — witty, but profane, no doubt.
Where 's *Cotton Mather ?*   he was always here. —
And so he would be, but he died last year.
Who is this preacher our Northampton claims,
Whose rhetoric blazes with sulphureous flames
And torches stolen from Tartarean mines ?
Edwards, the salamander of divines.
A deep, strong nature, pure and undefiled ;
Faith, firm as his who stabbed his sleeping child ;
Alas for him who blindly strays apart
And seeking God has lost his human heart !
Fall where they might no flying cinders caught
These sober halls where WADSWORTH ruled and
      taught.

One footstep more ; the fourth receding stride
Leaves the round century on the nearer side.

GOD SAVE KING CHARLES! God knows that pleas-
    ant knave
His grace will find it hard enough to save.
Ten years and more, and now the Plague, the Fire,
Talk of all tongues, at last begin to tire;
One fear prevails, all other frights forgot, —
White lips are whispering, — hark! *The popish
    Plot!*
Happy New England, from such troubles free
In health and peace beyond the stormy sea!
No Romish daggers threat her children's throats,
No gibbering nightmare mutters " *Titus Oates;* "
Philip is slain, the Quaker graves are green,
Not yet the witch has entered on the scene;
Happy our Harvard; pleased her graduates four;
URIAN OAKES the name their parchments bore.

  Two centuries past, our hurried feet arrive
At the last footprint of the scanty five;
Take the fifth stride; our wandering eyes explore
A tangled forest on a trackless shore;
Here, where we stand, the savage sorcerer howls,
The wild cat snarls, the stealthy gray wolf prowls,
The slouching bear, perchance the trampling moose
Starts the brown squaw and scares her red pap-
    poose;
At every step the lurking foe is near;
His Demons reign; God has no temple here!

Lift up your eyes! behold these pictured walls;
Look where the flood of western glory falls
Through the great sunflower disk of blazing panes
In ruby, saffron, azure, emerald stains;
With reverent step the marble pavement tread
Where our proud Mother's martyr-roll is read;
See the great halls that cluster, gathering round
This lofty shrine with holiest memories crowned;
See the fair Matron in her summer bower;
Fresh as a rose in bright perennial flower;
Read on her standard, always in the van,
"TRUTH," — the one word that makes a slave a
    man;
Think whose the hands that fed her altar-fires,
Then count the debt we owe our scholar-sires!

Brothers, farewell! the fast declining ray
Fades to the twilight of our golden day;
Some lesson yet our wearied brains may learn,
Some leaves, perhaps, in life's thin volume turn.
How few they seem as in our waning age
We count them backwards to the title-page!
Oh let us trust with holy men of old
Not all the story here begun is told;
So the tired spirit, waiting to be freed,
On life's last leaf with tranquil eye shall read
By the pale glimmer of the torch reversed,
Not *Finis*, but *The End of Volume First!*

MY AVIARY.

Through my north window, in the wintry weath-
    er, —
  My airy oriel on the river shore, —
I watch the sea-fowl as they flock together
  Where late the boatman flashed his dripping oar.

The gull, high floating, like a sloop unladen,
  Lets the loose water waft him as it will;
The duck, round-breasted as a rustic maiden,
  Paddles and plunges, busy, busy still.

I see the solemn gulls in council sitting
  On some broad ice-floe, pondering long and late,
While overhead the home-bound ducks are flitting,
  And leave the tardy conclave in debate,

Those weighty questions in their breasts revolv-
    ing
  Whose deeper meaning science never learns,
Till at some reverend elder's look dissolving,
  The speechless senate silently adjourns.

2

But when along the waves the shrill north-easter
  Shrieks through the laboring coaster's shrouds
    " Beware ! "
The pale bird, kindling like a Christmas feaster
  When some wild chorus shakes the vinous air,

Flaps from the leaden wave in fierce rejoicing,
  Feels heaven's dumb lightning thrill his torpid
    nerves,
Now on the blast his whistling plumage poising,
  Now wheeling, whirling in fantastic curves.

Such is our gull ; a gentleman of leisure,
  Less fleshed than feathered ; bagged you 'll find
    him such ;
His virtue silence ; his employment pleasure ;
  Not bad to look at, and not good for much.

What of our duck ? He has some high-bred cousins, —
  His Grace the Canvas-back, My Lord the Brant, —
Anas and *Anser*, — both served up by dozens,
  At Boston's *Rocher*, half-way to Nahant.

As for himself, he seems alert and thriving, —
  Grubs up a living somehow — what, who knows ?
Crabs ? mussels ? weeds ? — Look quick ! there 's one
    just diving !
  Flop ! Splash ! his white breast glistens — down
    he goes !

And while he 's under — just about a minute —
　　I take advantage of the fact to say
His fishy carcase has no virtue in it
　　The gunning idiot's worthless hire to pay.

He knows you ! " sportsmen " from suburban alleys,
　　Stretched under seaweed in the treacherous punt;
Knows every lazy, shiftless lout that sallies
　　Forth to waste powder — as *he* says, to " hunt."

I watch you with a patient satisfaction,
　　Well pleased to discount your predestined luck;
The float that figures in your sly transaction
　　Will carry back a goose, but not a duck.

Shrewd is our bird; not easy to outwit him !
　　Sharp is the outlook of those pin-head eyes;
Still, he is mortal and a shot may hit him,
　　One cannot always miss him if he tries.

Look! there 's a young one, dreaming not of danger;
　　Sees a flat log come floating down the stream;
Stares undismayed upon the harmless stranger;
　　Ah ! were all strangers harmless as they seem !

Habet ! a leaden shower his breast has shattered;
　　Vainly he flutters, not again to rise;
His soft white plumes along the waves are scattered;
　　Helpless the wing that braved the tempest lies.

He sees his comrades high above him flying
　　To seek their nests among the island reeds;
Strong is their flight; all lonely he is lying
　　Washed by the crimsoned water as he bleeds.

O Thou who carest for the falling sparrow,
　　Canst Thou the sinless sufferer's pang forget?
Or is Thy dread account-book's page so narrow
　　Its one long column scores Thy creatures' debt?

Poor gentle guest, by nature kindly cherished,
　　A world grows dark with thee in blinding death;
One little gasp — thy universe has perished,
　　Wrecked by the idle thief who stole thy breath!

Is this the whole sad story of creation,
　　Lived by its breathing myriads o'er and o'er, —
One glimpse of day, then black annihilation, —
　　A sunlit passage to a sunless shore?

Give back our faith, ye mystery-solving lynxes!
　　Robe us once more in heaven-aspiring creeds!
Happier was dreaming Egypt with her sphynxes,
　　The stony convent with its cross and beads!

How often gazing where a bird reposes,
　　Rocked on the wavelets, drifting with the tide,
I lose myself in strange metempsychosis
　　And float a sea-fowl at a sea-fowl's side,

From rain, hail, snow in feathery mantle muffled,
   Clear-eyed, strong-limbed, with keenest sense to
       hear
My mate soft murmuring, who, with plumes unruffled,
   Where'er I wander still is nestling near;

The great blue hollow like a garment o'er me;
   Space all unmeasured, unrecorded time;
While seen with inward eye moves on before me
   Thought's pictured train in wordless pantomime.

— A voice recalls me. — From my window turning
   I find myself a plumeless biped still;
No beak, no claws, no sign of wings discerning, —
   In fact with nothing bird-like but my quill.

ON THE THRESHOLD.

INTRODUCTION TO A COLLECTION OF POEMS BY
DIFFERENT AUTHORS.

An usher standing at the door
  I show my white rosette ;
A smile of welcome, nothing more,
  Will pay my trifling debt ;
Why should I bid you idly wait
Like lovers at the swinging gate ?

Can I forget the wedding guest ?
  The veteran of the sea ?
In vain the listener smites his breast, —
  " There was a ship " cries he !
Poor fasting victim, stunned and pale
He needs must listen to the tale.

He sees the gilded throng within,
  The sparkling goblets gleam,
The music and the merry din
  Through every window stream,
But there he shivers in the cold
Till all the crazy dream is told.

Not mine the graybeard's glittering eye
   That held his captive still
To hold my silent prisoners by
   And let me have my will;
Nay, *I* were like the three-years' child,
To think you could be so beguiled!

My verse is but the curtain's fold
   That hides the painted scene,
The mist by morning's ray unrolled
   That veils the meadow's green,
The cloud that needs must drift away
To show the rose of opening day.

See, from the tinkling rill you hear
   In hollowed palm I bring
These scanty drops, but ah, how near
   The founts that heavenward spring!
Thus, open wide the gates are thrown
And founts and flowers are all your own!

TO GEORGE PEABODY.

DANVERS, 1866.

BANKRUPT! our pockets inside out!
  Empty of words to speak his praises!
Worcester and Webster up the spout!
  Dead broke of laudatory phrases!
Yet why with flowery speeches tease,
  With vain superlatives distress him?
Has language better words than these?
  THE FRIEND OF ALL HIS RACE, GOD BLESS HIM!

A simple prayer — but words more sweet
  By human lips were never uttered,
Since Adam left the country seat
  Where angel wings around him fluttered.
The old look on with tear-dimmed eyes,
  The children cluster to caress him,
And every voice unbidden cries
  THE FRIEND OF ALL HIS RACE, GOD BLESS HIM!

AT THE PAPYRUS CLUB.

A LOVELY show for eyes to see
    I looked upon this morning —
A bright-hued, feathered company
    Of nature's own adorning ;
But ah ! those minstrels would not sing
    A listening ear while I lent —
The lark sat still and preened his wing —
    The nightingale was silent ;
I longed for what they gave me not —
    Their warblings sweet and fluty,
But grateful still for all I got
    I thanked them for their beauty.

A fairer vision meets my view
    Of Claras, Margarets, Marys,
In silken robes of varied hue,
    Like bluebirds and canaries —
The roses blush, the jewels gleam,
    The silks and satins glisten,
The black eyes flash, the blue eyes beam,
    We look — and then we listen :

Behold the flock we cage to-night —
   Was ever such a capture?
To see them is a pure delight —
   To hear them — ah! what rapture!

Methinks I hear Delilah's laugh
   At Samson bound in fetters; —
" *We* captured!" shrieks each lovelier half,
   " Men think themselves *our* betters!
We push the bolt, we turn the key
   On warriors, poets, sages,
Too happy, all of them, to be
   Locked in our golden cages!"

Beware! the boy with bandaged eyes
   Has flung away his blinder;
He 's lost his mother — so he cries —
   And here he knows he 'll find her:
The rogue! 't is but a new device —
   Look out for flying arrows
Whene'er the birds of Paradise
   Are perched amid the sparrows!

FOR WHITTIER'S SEVENTIETH BIRTHDAY.

DECEMBER 17, 1877.

I BELIEVE that the copies of verses I 've spun,
Like Scheherazade's tales, are a thousand and one, —
You remember the story, — those mornings in bed, —
'T was the turn of a copper, — a tale or a head.

A doom like Scheherazade's falls upon me
In a mandate as stern as the Sultan's decree :
I 'm a florist in verse, and what *would* people say
If I came to a banquet without my bouquet ?

It is trying, no doubt, when the company knows
Just the look and the smell of each lily and rose,
The green of each leaf in the sprigs that I bring,
And the shape of the bunch and the knot of the
     string.

Yes, — " the style is the man," and the nib of one's
     pen
Makes the same mark at twenty, and three-score
     and ten ;

It is so in all matters, if truth may be told;
Let one look at the cast he can tell you the mould.

How we all know each other ! no use in disguise ;
Through the holes in the mask comes the flash of
    the eyes;
We can tell by his — somewhat — each one of our
    tribe,
As we know the old hat which we cannot describe.

Though in Hebrew, in Sanscrit, in Choctaw you
    write,
Sweet singer who gave us the Voices of Night,
Though in buskin or slipper your song may be shod,
Or the velvety verse that Evangeline trod,

We shall say " You can't cheat us, — we know it is
    you,"
There is one voice like that, but there cannot be two,
Maë'stro, whose chant like the dulcimer rings :
And the woods will be hushed while the nightingale
    sings.

And he, so serene, so majestic, so true,
Whose temple hypæthral the planets shine through,
Let us catch but five words from that mystical pen,
We should know our one sage from all children of
    men.

And he whose bright image no distance can dim,
Through a hundred disguises we can't mistake him,
Whose play is all earnest, whose wit is the edge
(With a beetle behind) of a sham-splitting wedge.

Do you know whom we send you, Hidalgos of
    Spain ?
Do you know your old friends when you see them
    again ?
Hosea was Sancho! you Dons of Madrid,
But Sancho that wielded the lance of the Cid !

And the wood-thrush of Essex, — you know whom I
    mean,
Whose song echoes round us while he sits unseen,
Whose heart-throbs of verse through our memories
    thrill
Like a breath from the wood, like a breeze from the
    hill,

So fervid, so simple, so loving, so pure,
We hear but one strain and our verdict is sure, —
Thee cannot elude us, — no further we search, —
'T is Holy George Herbert cut loose from his church!

We think it the voice of a seraph that sings, —
Alas ! we remember that angels have wings, —
What story is this of the day of his birth ?
Let him live to a hundred! we want him on earth !

One life has been paid him (in gold) by the sun ;
One account has been squared and another begun ;
But he never will die if he lingers below
Till we've paid him in love half the balance we
    owe !

TWO SONNETS: HARVARD.[1]

"CHRISTO ET ECCLESIÆ." 1700.

To God's anointed and his chosen flock :
  So ran the phrase the black-robed conclave chose
  To guard the sacred cloisters that arose
Like David's altar on Moriah's rock.
Unshaken still those ancient arches mock
  The ram's-horn summons of the windy foes
  Who stand like Joshua's army while it blows
And wait to see them toppling with the shock.
Christ and the Church. *Their* church, whose nar-
    row door
  Shut out the many, who if over bold
  Like hunted wolves were driven from the fold,
Bruised with the flails those godly zealots bore,
  Mindful that Israel's altar stood of old
Where echoed once Araunah's threshing-floor.

[1] At the meeting of the New York Harvard Club, February 21, 1878.

1643. "VERITAS." 1878.

TRUTH: So the frontlet's older legend ran,
  On the brief record's opening page displayed ;
  Not yet those clear-eyed scholars were afraid
Lest the fair fruit that wrought the woe of man
By far Euphrates, — where our sire began
  His search for truth, and seeking, was betrayed,—
  Might work new treason in their forest shade,
Doubling the curse that brought life's shortened
      span.
Nurse of the future, daughter of the past,
  That stern phylactery best becomes thee now :
  Lift to the morning star thy marble brow !
Cast thy brave truth on every warring blast !
  Stretch thy white hand to that forbidden bough,
And let thine earliest symbol be thy last !

THE LAST SURVIVOR.[1]

Yes! the vacant chairs tell sadly we are going, going
    fast,
And the thought comes strangely o'er me who will
    live to be the last?
When the twentieth century's sunbeams climb the
    far-off eastern hill
With his ninety winters burdened will he greet the
    morning still?

Will he stand with Harvard's nurslings when they
    hear their mother's call
And the old and young are gathered in the many al-
    coved hall?
Will he answer to the summons when they range
    themselves in line
And the young mustachioed marshal calls out " Class
    of 29 " ?

Methinks I see the column as its lengthened ranks
    appear
In the sunshine of the morrow of the nineteen hun-
    dredth year;

[1] Annual meeting of the Class of 1829, January 10, 1878.

Through the yard 't is creeping, winding, by the walls
    of dusky red —
What shape is that which totters at the long proces-
    sion's head ?

Who knows this ancient graduate of fourscore years
    and ten, —
What place he held, what name he bore among the
    sons of men ?
So speeds the curious question ; its answer travels slow ;
" 'T is the last of sixty classmates of seventy years
    ago."

His figure shows but dimly, his face I scarce can see, —
There 's something that reminds me, — it looks like
    — is it he ?
He? Who? No voice may whisper what wrinkled
    brow shall claim
The wreath of stars that circles our last survivor's
    name.

Will he be some veteran minstrel, left to pipe in fee-
    ble rhyme
All the stories and the glories of our gay and golden
    time ?
Or some quiet, voiceless brother in whose lonely lov-
    ing breast
Fond memory broods in silence, like a dove upon her
    nest ?

Will it be some old *Emeritus*, who taught so long
      ago
The boys that heard him lecture have heads as white
      as snow ?
Or a pious, painful preacher, holding forth from year
      to year
Till his colleague got a colleague whom the young
      folks flocked to hear ?

Will it be a rich old merchant in a square-tied white
      cravat,
Or select-man of a village in a pre-historic hat?
Will his dwelling be a mansion in a marble-fronted
      row,
Or a homestead by a hillside where the huckleberries
      grow ?

I can see our one survivor, sitting lonely by himself, —
All his college text-books round him, ranged in order
      on their shelf ;
There are classic "interliners" filled with learning's
      choicest pith,
Each *cum notis variorum, quas recensuit doctus*
      Smith ;

Physics, metaphysics, logic, mathematics — all the
      lot —
Every wisdom-crammed octavo he has mastered and
      forgot,

With the ghosts of dead Professors standing guard
    beside them all;
And the room is full of shadows which their lettered
    backs recall.

How the past spreads out in vision with its far reced-
    ing train,
Like a long embroidered arras in the chambers of the
    brain,
From opening manhood's morning when first we
    learned to grieve
To the fond regretful moments of our sorrow sad-
    dened eve!

What early shadows darkened our idle summer's
    joy
When death snatched roughly from us that lovely
    bright-eyed boy![1]
The years move swiftly onwards; the deadly shafts
    fall fast, —
Till all have dropped around him — lo, there he
    stands, — the last!

Their faces flit before him, some rosy-hued and
    fair,
Some strong in iron manhood, some worn with toil
    and care, —

[1] William Sturgis.

Their smiles no more shall greet him on cheeks with
    pleasure flushed !
The friendly hands are folded, the pleasant voices
    hushed !

.   .   .   .

My picture sets me dreaming; alas ! and can it be
Those two familiar faces we never more may see ?
In every entering footfall I think them drawing near,
With every door that opens I say, "At last they 're
    here ! "

The willow bends unbroken when angry tempests
    blow,
The stately oak is levelled and all its strength laid
    low;
So fell that tower of manhood, undaunted, patient,
    strong,
White with the gathering snow-flakes, who faced the
    storm so long.[1]

And he,[2] — what subtle phrases their varying lights
    must blend
To paint as each remembers our many-featured
    friend !
His wit a flash auroral that laughed in every look,
His talk a sunbeam broken on the ripples of a brook,

[1] Francis B. Crowninshield.   [2] George T. Davis.

Or, fed from thousand sources, a fountain's glittering
  jet,
Or careless handfuls scattered of diamond sparks un-
  set,
Ah, sketch him, paint him, mould him in every shape
  you will,
He was *himself* — the only — the one unpictured
  still !

Farewell ! our skies are darkened and yet the stars
  will shine,
We 'll close our ranks together and still fall into line
Till one is left, one only, to mourn for all the rest ;
And Heaven bequeath their memories to him who
  loves us best !

THE ARCHBISHOP AND GIL BLAS.[1]

A MODERNIZED VERSION.

I DON'T think I feel much older; I'm aware I'm
     rather gray,
But so are many young folks; I meet 'em every day.
I confess I'm more particular in what I eat and
     drink,
But one's taste improves with culture; that is all
     it means, I think.

Can you read as once you used to? Well, the print-
     ing is so bad,
No young folks' eyes can read it like the books that
     once we had.
Are you quite as quick of hearing? Please to say
     that once again.
Don't I use plain words, your Reverence? Yes, I
     often use a cane,

But it's not because I need it, — no, I always liked a
     stick;
And as one might lean upon it, 't is as well it should
     be thick.

[1] Annual Meeting of the Class of 1829, January 6, 1879.

Oh, I 'm smart, I 'm spry, I 'm lively, — I can walk,
    yes, that I can,
On the days I feel like walking, just as well as you,
    young man !

Don't you get a little sleepy after dinner every
    day ?
Well, I doze a little, sometimes, but that always was
    my way.
Don't you cry a little easier than some twenty years
    ago ?
Well, my heart is very tender, but I think 't was
    always so.

Don't you find it sometimes happens that you can't
    recall a name ?
Yes, — I know such lots of people, — but my mem-
    ory 's not to blame.
What! You think my memory 's failing! Why,
    it 's just as bright and clear, —
I remember my great-grandma! She 's been dead
    these sixty year !

Is your voice a little trembly ? Well, it may be,
    now and then,
But I write as well as ever with a good old-fashioned
    pen ;

It 's the Gillotts make the trouble, — not at all my
finger-ends, —
That is why my hand looks shaky when I sign for
dividends.

Don't you stoop a little, walking ? It 's a way I 've
always had —
I have always been round-shouldered ever since I
was a lad.
Don't you hate to tie your shoe-strings ? Yes, I own
it — that is true.
Don't you tell old stories over ? I am not aware
I do.

*Don't you stay at home of evenings ? Don't you love
a cushioned seat
In a corner, by the fireside, with your slippers on
your feet ?
Don't you wear warm fleecy flannels ? Don't you
muffle up your throat ?
Don't you like to have one help you when you 're put-
ting on your coat ?*

*Don't you like old books you 've dogs-eared, you can't
remember when ?
Don't you call it late at nine o'clock and go to bed at
ten ?*

How many cronies can you count of all you used to know
Who called you by your Christian name some fifty years ago?

How look the prizes to you that used to fire your brain?
You 've reared your mound — how high is it above the level plain?
You 've drained the brimming golden cup that made your fancy reel,
You 've slept the giddy potion off, — now tell us how you feel!

You 've watched the harvest ripening till every stem was cropped,
You 've seen the rose of beauty fade till every petal dropped,
You 've told your thought, you 've done your task, you 've tracked your dial round,
— I backing down! Thank Heaven, not yet! I 'm hale and brisk and sound,

And good for many a tussle, as you shall live to see ;
My shoes are not quite ready yet — don't think you 're rid of me !

Old Parr was in his lusty prime when he was older
    far,
And where will you be if I live to beat old Thomas
    Parr ?

Ah well, — I know, — at every age life has a certain
    charm, —
You're going ?   Come, permit me, please, I beg you'll
    take my arm.
I take your arm !   Why take your arm ? I 'd thank
    you to be told ;
I 'm old enough to walk alone, but not so *very* old !

THE SHADOWS.[1]

"How many have gone?" was the question of old
  Ere time our bright ring of its jewels bereft;
Alas! for too often the death-bell has tolled,
  And the question we ask is, "How many are
    left?"

Bright sparkled the wine; there were *fifty* that
    quaffed;
  For a decade had slipped and had taken but three;
How they frolicked and sung, — how they shouted
    and laughed,
  Like a school full of boys from their benches set
    free!

There were speeches and toasts, there were stories
    and rhymes,
  The hall shook its sides with their merriment's
    noise;

[1] Annual Meeting of the Class of 1829, January 8, 1880.

As they talked and lived over the college-day
    times, —
  No wonder they kept their old name of " The
    Boys ! "

The seasons moved on in their rhythmical flow
  With mornings like maidens that pouted or
    smiled,
With the bud and the leaf and the fruit and the
    snow,
  And the year-books of Time in his alcoves were
    piled.

There were *forty* that gathered where fifty had
    met ;
  Some locks had got silvered, some lives had grown
    sere,
But the laugh of the laughers was lusty as yet,
  And the song of the singers rose ringing and
    clear.

Still flitted the years ; there were *thirty* that came ;
  " The Boys " they were still and they answered
    their call ;
There were foreheads of care, but the smiles were
    the same
  And the chorus rang loud through the garlanded
    hall.

The hour-hand moved on, and they gathered again ;
  There were *twenty* that joined in the hymn that
    was sung,
But ah ! for our song-bird we listened in vain,—
  The crystalline tones like a seraph's that rung !

How narrow the circle that holds us to-night !
  How many the loved ones that greet us no more,
As we meet like the stragglers that come from the
    fight,
  Like the mariners flung from a wreck on the
    shore !

We look through the twilight for those we have
    lost ;
  The stream rolls between us and yet they seem
    near ;
Already outnumbered by those who have crossed,
  Our band is transplanted, its home is not here !

They smile on us still — is it only a dream ? —
  While fondly or proudly their names we recall —
They beckon — they come — they are crossing the
    stream —
  Lo ! the Shadows ! the Shadows ! room — room for
    them all !

THE COMING ERA.

THEY tell us that the Muse is soon to fly hence,
  Leaving the bowers of song that were once dear,
Her robes bequeathing to her sister, Science,
  The groves of Pindus for the axe to clear.

Optics will claim the wandering eye of fancy,
  Physics will grasp imagination's wings,
Plain fact exorcise fiction's necromancy,
  The workshop hammer where the minstrel sings.

No more with laughter at Thalia's frolics
  Our eyes shall twinkle till the tears run down,
But in her place the lecturer on hydraulics
  Spout forth his watery science to the town.

No more our foolish passions and affections
  The tragic Muse with mimic grief shall try,
But, nobler far, a course of vivisections
  Teach what it costs a tortured brute to die.

The unearthed monad, long in buried rocks hid,
  Shall tell the secret whence our being came;

The chemist show us death is life's black oxide,
  Left when the breath no longer fans its flame.

Instead of cracked-brained poets in their attics
  Filling thin volumes with their flowery talk,
There shall be books of wholesome mathematics;
  The tutor with his blackboard and his chalk.

No longer bards with madrigal and sonnet
  Shall woo to moonlight walks the ribboned sex,
But side by side the beaver and the bonnet
  Stroll, calmly pondering on some problem's x.

The sober bliss of serious calculation
  Shall mock the trivial joys that fancy drew,
And, oh, the rapture of a solved equation, —
  One self-same answer on the lips of two!

So speak in solemn tones our youthful sages,
  Patient, severe, laborious, slow, exact,
As o'er creation's protoplasmic pages
  They browse and munch the thistle crops of fact.

And yet we 've sometimes found it rather pleasant
  To dream again the scenes that Shakespeare
    drew, —
To walk the hill-side with the Scottish peasant
  Among the daisies wet with morning's dew;

To leave awhile the daylight of the real,
   Led by the guidance of the master's hand,
For the strange radiance of the far ideal, —
   " The light that never was on sea or land."

Well, Time alone can lift the future's curtain, —
   Science may teach our children all she knows,
But love will kindle fresh young hearts, 't is certain,
   And June will not forget her blushing rose.

And so, in spite of all that Time is bringing, —
   Treasures of truth and miracles of art,
Beauty and Love will keep the poet singing,
   And song still live, — the science of the heart.

IN RESPONSE.[1]

SUCH kindness! the scowl of a cynic would soften,
  His pulse beat its way to some eloquent word, —
Alas! my poor accents have echoed too often,
  Like that Pinafore music you 've some of you
    heard.

Do you know me, dear strangers — the hundredth-
    time comer
  At banquets and feasts since the days of my Spring?
Ah! would I could borrow one rose of my Summer,
  But this is a leaf of my Autumn I bring.

I look at your faces, — I 'm sure there are some from
  The three-breasted mother I count as my own;
You think you remember the place you have come
    from,
  But how it has changed in the years that have
    flown!.

Unaltered, 't is true, is the hall we call " Funnel ; "
  Still fights the " Old South " in the battle for life,

[1] Breakfast at the Century Club, New York, May, 1879.

But we 've opened our door to the West through the
    tunnel,
  And we 've cut off Fort Hill with our Amazon
    knife.

You should see the new Westminster Boston has
    builded, —
  Its mansions, its spires, its museums of arts, —
You should see the great dome we have gorgeously
    gilded, —
  'T is the light of our eyes, 't is the joy of our hearts.

When first in his path a young asteroid found it,
  As he sailed through the skies with the stars in his
    wake,
He thought 't was the sun, and kept circling around
    it
  Till Edison signalled, " You 've made a mistake."

We are proud of our city — her fast-growing figure —
  The warp and the woof of her brain and her
    hands, —
But we 're proudest of all that her heart has grown
    bigger,
  And warms with fresh blood as her girdle expands.

One lesson the rubric of conflict has taught her :
  Though parted awhile by war's earth-rending
    shock,

The lines that divide us are written in water,
    The love that unites us cut deep in the rock.

As well might the Judas of treason endeavor
    To write his black name on the disk of the sun
As try the bright star-wreath that binds us to sever
    And blot the fair legend of " Many in One."

We love YOU, tall sister, the stately, the splendid, —
    The banner of empire floats high on your towers,
Yet ever in welcome your arms are extended, —
    We share in your splendors, your glory is ours.

Yes, Queen of the Continent ! All of us own thee, —
    The gold-freighted argosies flock at thy call, —
The naiads, the sea-nymphs have met to enthrone
        thee,
    But the Broadway of one is the Highway of all!

— I thank you. Three words that can hardly be
        mended,
    Though phrases on phrases their eloquence pile,
If you hear the heart's throb with their syllables
        blended,
    And read all they mean in a sunshiny smile.

FOR THE MOORE CENTENNIAL CELEBRA-
TION.

MAY 28, 1879.

I.

ENCHANTER of Erin, whose magic has bound us,
  Thy wand for one moment we fondly would claim,
Entranced while it summons the phantoms around us
  That blush into life at the sound of thy name.

The tell-tales of memory wake from their slum-
      bers, —
  I hear the old song with its tender refrain, —
What passion lies hid in those honey-voiced numbers!
  What perfume of youth in each exquisite strain!

The home of my childhood comes back as a vision, —
  Hark! Hark! A soft chord from its song-haunted
      room, —
'T is a morning of May, when the air is Elysian, —
  The syringa in bud and the lilac in bloom, —

We are clustered around the " Clementi " piano, —
  There were six of us then, — there are two of us
      now,—

She is singing, — the girl with the silver soprano, —
  How " The Lord of the Valley " was false to his
    vow:

" Let Erin remember " the echoes are calling :
  Through " The Vale of Avoca " the waters are
    rolled:
" The Exile " laments while the night-dews are fall-
    ing :
  " The Morning of Life " dawns again as of old.

But ah ! those warm love-songs of fresh adolescence !
  Around us such raptures celestial they flung
That it seemed as if Paradise breathed its quintes-
    sence
  Through the seraph-toned lips of the maiden that
    sung !

Long hushed are the chords that my boyhood en-
    chanted
  As when the smooth wave by the angel was
    stirred,
Yet still with their music is memory haunted
  And oft in my dreams are their melodies heard.

I feel like the priest to his altar returning, —
  The crowd that was kneeling no longer is there,

The flame has died down, but the brands are still
    burning,
  And sandal and cinnamon sweeten the air.

II.

The veil for her bridal young Summer is weaving
  In her azure-domed hall with its tapestried floor,
And Spring the last tear-drops of May-dew is leaving
  On the daisy of Burns and the shamrock of
    Moore.

How like, how unlike, as we view them together,
  The song of the minstrels whose record we scan, —
One fresh as the breeze blowing over the heather, —
  One sweet as the breath from an odalisque's fan!

Ah, passion can glow mid a palace's splendor;
  The cage does not alter the song of the bird;
And the curtain of silk has known whispers as tender
  As ever the blossoming hawthorn has heard.

No fear lest the step of the soft-slippered Graces
  Should fright the young Loves from their warm
    little nest,
For the heart of a queen, under jewels and laces,
  Beats time with the pulse in the peasant girl's
    breast!

Thrice welcome each gift of kind Nature's bestow-
　　ing !
　　Her fountain heeds little the goblet we hold ;
Alike, when its musical waters are flowing,
　　The shell from the seaside, the chalice of gold.

The twins of the lyre to her voices had listened ;
　　Both laid their best gifts upon Liberty's shrine ;
For Coila's loved minstrel the holly-wreath glist-
　　ened ;
　　For Erin's the rose and the myrtle entwine.

And while the fresh blossoms of summer are braided
　　For the sea-girdled, stream-silvered, lake-jewelled
　　　isle,
While her mantle of verdure is woven unfaded,
　　While Shannon and Liffey shall dimple and smile,

The land where the staff of Saint Patrick was
　　planted,
　　Where the shamrock grows green from the cliffs
　　　to the shore,
The land of fair maidens and heroes undaunted,
　　Shall wreathe her bright harp with the garlands
　　　of Moore !

TO JAMES FREEMAN CLARKE.

APRIL 4, 1880.

I BRING the simplest pledge of love,
    Friend of my earlier days ;
Mine is the hand without the glove,
    The heart-beat, not the phrase.

How few still breathe this mortal air
    We called by schoolboy names !
You still, whatever robe you wear,
    To me are always James.

That name the kind apostle bore
    Who shames the sullen creeds,
Not trusting less, but loving more,
    And showing faith by deeds.

What blending thoughts our memories share !
    What visions yours and mine
Of May-days in whose morning air
    The dews were golden wine,

Of vistas bright with opening day,
    Whose all-awakening sun
Showed in life's landscape, far away,
    The summits to be won!

The heights are gained. — Ah, say not so
    For him who smiles at time,
Leaves his tired comrades down below,
    And only lives to climb!

His labors, — will they ever cease, —
    With hand and tongue and pen?
Shall wearied Nature ask release
    At threescore years and ten?

Our strength the clustered seasons tax, —
    For him new life they mean;
Like rods around the lictor's axe
    They keep him bright and keen.

The wise, the brave, the strong, we know, —
    We mark them here or there,
But he, — we roll our eyes, and lo!
    We find him everywhere!

With truth's bold cohorts, or alone,
    He strides through error's field;
His lance is ever manhood's own,
    His breast is woman's shield.

Count not his years while earth has need
   Of souls that Heaven inflames
With sacred zeal to save, to lead, —
   Long live our dear Saint James !

WELCOME TO THE CHICAGO COMMERCIAL CLUB.

JANUARY 14, 1880.

CHICAGO sounds rough to the maker of verse ;
One comfort we have — Cincinnati sounds worse ;
If we only were licensed to say Chicagó !
But Worcester and Webster won't let us, you know.

No matter, we songsters must sing as we can ;
We can make some nice couplets with Lake Michi-
      gan,
And what more resembles a nightingale's voice,
Than the oily trisyllable, sweet Illinois ?

Your waters are fresh, while our harbor is salt,
But we know you can't help it — it is n't your fault ;
Our city is old and your city is new,
But the railroad men tell us we 're greener than you.

You have seen our gilt dome, and no doubt you 've
      been told
That the orbs of the universe round it are rolled ;

But I 'll own it to you, and I ought to know best,
That this is n't quite true of all stars of the West.

You 'll go to Mount Auburn — we 'll show you the
    track, —
And can stay there, — unless you prefer to come
    back ;
And Bunker's tall shaft you can climb if you will,
But you 'll puff like a paragraph praising a pill.

You must see — but you *have* seen — our old Fan-
    euil Hall,
Our churches, our school-rooms, our sample-rooms,
    all ;
And, perhaps, though the idiots must have their jokes,
You have found our good people much like other folks.

There are cities by rivers, by lakes and by seas,
Each as full of itself as a cheese-mite of cheese ;
And a city will brag as a game-cock will crow :
Don't your cockerels at home — just a little, you
    know ?

But we 'll crow for you now — here 's a health to the
    boys,
Men, maidens, and matrons of fair Illinois,
And the rainbow of friendship that arches its span
From the green of the sea to the blue Michigan !

AMERICAN ACADEMY CENTENNIAL CELEBRATION.

MAY 26, 1880.

SIRE, son, and grandson ; so the century glides ;
    Three lives, three strides, three footprints in the
        sand ;
Silent as midnight's falling meteor slides
    Into the stillness of the far-off land ;
    How dim the space its little arc has spanned !

See on this opening page the names renowned
    Tombed in these records on our dusty shelves,
Scarce on the scroll of living memory found,
    Save where the wan-eyed antiquarian delves ;
    Shadows they seem ; ah, what are we ourselves ?

Pale ghosts of Bowdoin, Winthrop, Willard, West,
    Sages of busy brain and wrinkled brow,
Searchers of Nature's secrets unconfessed,
    Asking of all things Whence and Why and How —
    What problems meet your larger vision now ?

Has Gannett tracked the wild Aurora's path?
　Has Bowdoin found his all-surrounding sphere?
What question puzzles ciphering Philomath?
　Could Williams make the hidden causes clear
　Of the Dark Day that filled the land with fear?

Dear ancient schoolboys!   Nature taught to them
　The simple lessons of the star and flower,
Showed them strange sights; how on a single stem, —
　Admire the marvels of Creative Power! —
　Twin apples grew, one sweet, the other sour,

How from the hill-top where our eyes behold
　In even ranks the plumed and bannered maize
Range its long columns, in the days of old
　The live volcano shot its angry blaze, —
　Dead since the showers of Noah's watery days;

How, when the lightning split the mighty rock,
　The spreading fury of the shaft was spent;
How the young scion joined the alien stock,
　And when and where the homeless swallows went
　To pass the winter of their discontent.

Scant were the gleanings in those years of dearth;
　No Cuvier yet had clothed the fossil bones
That slumbered, waiting for their second birth;
　No Lyell read the legend of the stones;
　Science still pointed to her empty thrones.

Dreaming of orbs to eyes of earth unknown,
    Herschel looked heavenwards in the starlight
        pale;
Lost in those awful depths he trod alone,
    Laplace stood mute before the lifted veil;
    While home-bred Humboldt trimmed his toy ship's
        sail.

No mortal feet these loftier heights had gained
    Whence the wide realms of Nature we descry;
In vain their eyes our longing fathers strained
    To scan with wondering gaze the summits high
    That far beneath their children's footpaths lie.

Smile at their first small ventures as we may,
    The school-boy's copy shapes the scholar's hand,
Their grateful memory fills our hearts to-day;
    Brave, hopeful, wise, this bower of peace they
        planned,
    While war's dread ploughshare scarred the suffer-
        ing land.

Child of our children's children yet unborn,
    When on this yellow page you turn your eyes,
Where the brief record of this May-day morn
    In phrase antique and faded letters lies,
    How vague, how pale our flitting ghosts will rise!

Yet in our veins the blood ran warm and red,
  For us the fields were green, the skies were blue,
Though from our dust the spirit long has fled,
  We lived, we loved, we toiled, we dreamed like
    you,
  Smiled at our sires and thought how much we
    knew.

Oh might our spirits for one hour return,
  When the next century rounds its hundredth ring,
All the strange secrets it shall teach to learn,
  To hear the larger truths its years shall bring,
  Its wiser sages talk, its sweeter minstrels sing!

THE SCHOOL-BOY.

READ AT THE CENTENNIAL CELEBRATION OF THE FOUNDATION
OF PHILLIPS ACADEMY, ANDOVER.

1778–1878.

THESE hallowed precincts, long to memory dear,
Smile with fresh welcome as our feet draw near ;
With softer gales the opening leaves are fanned,
With fairer hues the kindling flowers expand,
The rose-bush reddens with the blush of June,
The groves are vocal with their minstrels' tune,
The mighty elm, beneath whose arching shade
The wandering children of the forest strayed,
Greets the bright morning in its bridal dress,
And spreads its arms the gladsome dawn to bless.
　Is it an idle dream that nature shares
Our joys, our griefs, our pastimes, and our cares ?
Is there no summons when, at morning's call,
The sable vestments of the darkness fall?
Does not meek evening's low-voiced *Ave* blend
With the soft vesper as its notes ascend?
Is there no whisper in the perfumed air,
When the sweet bosom of the rose is bare ?

Does not the sunshine call us to rejoice ?
Is there no meaning in the storm-cloud's voice ?
No silent message when from midnight skies
Heaven looks upon us with its myriad eyes ?
　Or shift the mirror; say our dreams diffuse
O'er life's pale landscape their celestial hues,
Lend heaven the rainbow it has never known,
And robe the earth in glories not its own,
Sing their own music in the summer breeze,
With fresher foliage clothe the stately trees,
Stain the June blossoms with a livelier dye
And spread a bluer azure on the sky, —
Blest be the power that works its lawless will
And finds the weediest patch an Eden still;
No walls so fair as those our fancies build, —
No views so bright as those our visions gild!

　So ran my lines, as pen and paper met,
The truant goose-quill travelling like Planchette;
Too ready servant, whose deceitful ways
Full many a slipshod line, alas! betrays;
Hence of the rhyming thousand not a few
Have builded worse — a great deal — than they knew.

　What need of idle fancy to adorn
Our mother's birthplace on her birthday morn ?
Hers are the blossoms of eternal spring,
From these green boughs her new-fledged birds take
　　wing,

These echoes hear their earliest carols sung,
In this old nest the brood is ever young.
If some tired wanderer, resting from his flight,
Amid the gay young choristers alight,
These gather round him, mark his faded plumes
That faintly still the far-off grove perfumes,
And listen, wondering if some feeble note
Yet lingers, quavering in his weary throat: —
I, whose fresh voice yon red-faced temple knew,
What tune is left me, fit to sing to you?
Ask not the grandeurs of a labored song,
But let my easy couplets slide along;
Much could I tell you that you know too well;
Much I remember, but I will not tell;
Age brings experience; graybeards oft are wise,
But oh! how sharp a youngster's ears and eyes!

My cheek was bare of adolescent down
When first I sought the academic town;
Slow rolls the coach along the dusty road,
Big with its filial and parental load;
The frequent hills, the lonely woods are past,
The school-boy's chosen home is reached at last.
I see it now, the same unchanging spot,
The swinging gate, the little garden plot,
The narrow yard, the rock that made its floor,
The flat, pale house, the knocker-garnished door,
The small, trim parlor, neat, decorous, chill,
The strange, new faces, kind, but grave and still;

Two, creased with age,—or what I then called age,—
Life's volume open at its fiftieth page;
One, a shy maiden's, pallid, placid, sweet
As the first snow-drop which the sunbeams greet;
One the last nursling's; slight she was, and fair,
Her smooth white forehead warmed with auburn
      hair;
Last came the virgin Hymen long had spared,
Whose daily cares the grateful household shared,
Strong, patient, humble; her substantial frame
Stretched the chaste draperies I forbear to name.
   Brave, but with effort, had the school-boy come
To the cold comfort of a stranger's home;
How like a dagger to my sinking heart
Came the dry summons, " It is time to part;
" Good - by!" " Goo — ood - by!" one fond mater-
      nal kiss. . . . .
Homesick as death! Was ever pang like this? . . . .
Too young as yet with willing feet to stray
From the tame fireside, glad to get away,—
Too old to let my watery grief appear,—
And what so bitter as a swallowed tear!
   One figure still my vagrant thoughts pursue;
First boy to greet me, Ariel, where are you?
Imp of all mischief, heaven alone knows how
You learned it all,—are you an angel now,
Or tottering gently down the slope of years,
Your face grown sober in the vale of tears?

Forgive my freedom if you are breathing still;
If in a happier world, I know you will.
You were a school-boy — what beneath the sun
So like a monkey?   I was also one.

  Strange, sure enough, to see what curious shoots
The nursery raises from the study's roots!
In those old days the very, very good
Took up more room — a little — than they should;
Something too much one's eyes encountered then
Of serious youth and funeral-visaged men;
The solemn elders saw life's mournful half, —
Heaven sent this boy, whose mission was to laugh,
Drollest of buffos, Nature's odd protest,
A catbird squealing in a blackbird's nest.

  Kind, faithful Nature! While the sour-eyed
        Scot, —
Her cheerful smiles forbidden or forgot, —
Talks only of his preacher and his kirk, —
Hears five-hour sermons for his Sunday work, —
Praying and fasting till his meagre face
Gains its due length, the genuine sign of grace, —
An Ayrshire mother in the land of Knox
Her embryo poet in his cradle rocks; —
Nature, long shivering in her dim eclipse,
Steals in a sunbeam to those baby lips;
So to its home her banished smile returns,
And Scotland sweetens with the song of Burns!

The morning came; I reached the classic hall;
A clock-face eyed me, staring from the wall;
Beneath its hands a printed line I read:
YOUTH IS LIFE'S SEED-TIME: so the clock-face said:
Some took its council, as the sequel showed, —
Sowed, — their wild oats, — and reaped as they had
    sowed.

How all comes back! the upward slanting floor, —
The masters' thrones that flank the central door, —
The long, outstretching alleys that divide
The rows of desks that stand on either side, —
The staring boys, a face to every desk,
Bright, dull, pale, blooming, common, picturesque.

Grave is the Master's look; his forehead wears
Thick rows of wrinkles, prints of worrying cares;
Uneasy lie the heads of all that rule,
His most of all whose kingdom is a school.
Supreme he sits; before the awful frown
That bends his brows the boldest eye goes down;
Not more submissive Israel heard and saw
At Sinai's foot the Giver of the Law.

Less stern he seems, who sits in equal state
On the twin throne and shares the empire's weight;
Around his lips the subtle life that plays
Steals quaintly forth in many a jesting phrase;
A lightsome nature, not so hard to chafe,
Pleasant when pleased; rough-handled, not so safe;
Some tingling memories vaguely I recall,
But to forgive him.   God forgive us all!

One yet remains, whose well-remembered name
Pleads in my grateful heart its tender claim;
His was the charm magnetic, the bright look
That sheds its sunshine on the dreariest book;
A loving soul to every task he brought
That sweetly mingled with the lore he taught;
Sprung from a saintly race that never could
From youth to age be anything but good,
His few brief years in holiest labors spent,
Earth lost too soon the treasure heaven had lent.
Kindest of teachers, studious to divine
Some hint of promise in my earliest line,
These faint and faltering words thou can'st not hear
Throb from a heart that holds thy memory dear.

As to the traveller's eye the varied plain
Shows through the window of the flying train,
A mingled landscape, rather felt than seen,
A gravelly bank, a sudden flash of green,
A tangled wood, a glittering stream that flows
Through the cleft summit where the cliff once rose,
All strangely blended in a hurried gleam,
Rock, wood, waste, meadow, village, hill-side,
        stream, —
So, as we look behind us, life appears,
Seen through the vista of our bygone years.

Yet in the dead past's shadow-filled domain,
Some vanished shapes the hues of life retain;
Unbidden, oft, before our dreaming eyes
From the vague mists in memory's path they rise.

So comes his blooming image to my view,
The friend of joyous days when life was new,
Hope yet untamed, the blood of youth unchilled,
No blank arrear of promise unfulfilled,
Life's flower yet hidden in its sheltering fold,
Its pictured canvas yet to be unrolled.
His the frank smile I vainly look to greet,
His the warm grasp my clasping hand should
          meet;
How would our lips renew their schoolboy talk,
Our feet retrace the old familiar walk!
For thee no more earth's cheerful morning shines
Through the green fringes of the tented pines;
Ah me! is heaven so far thou canst not hear,
Or is thy viewless spirit hovering near,
A fair young presence, bright with morning's glow,
The fresh-cheeked boy of fifty years ago?

   Yes, fifty years, with all their circling suns,
Behind them all my glance reverted runs;
Where now that time remote, its griefs, its joys,
Where are its gray-haired men, its bright-haired
          boys?
Where is the patriarch time could hardly tire, —
The good old, wrinkled, immemorial "squire"?
(An honest treasurer, like a black-plumed swan,
Not every day our eyes may look upon.)
Where the tough champion who, with Calvin's sword,
In wordy conflicts battled for the Lord?

Where the grave scholar, lonely, calm, austere,
Whose voice like music charmed the listening ear,
Whose light rekindled, like the morning-star
Still shines upon us through the gates ajar?
Where the still, solemn, weary, sad-eyed man,
Whose care-worn face my wandering eyes would
    scan, —
His features wasted in the lingering strife
With the pale foe that drains the student's life?
Where my old friend, the scholar, teacher, saint,
Whose creed, some hinted, showed a speck of taint;
He broached his own opinion, which is not
Lightly to be forgiven or forgot;
Some riddle's point, — I scarce remember now, —
Homo*i*, perhaps, where they said homo — ou.
(If the unlettered greatly wish to know
Where lies the difference betwixt *oi* and *o*,
Those of the curious who have time may search
Among the stale conundrums of their church.)
Beneath his roof his peaceful life I shared,
And for his modes of faith I little cared, —
I, taught to judge men's dogmas by their deeds,
Long ere the days of india-rubber creeds.

    Why should we look one common faith to find,
Where one in every score is color-blind?
If here on earth they know not red from green,
Will they see better into things unseen!

Once more to time's old graveyard I return
And scrape the moss from memory's pictured urn.
Who, in these days when all things go by steam
Recalls the stage-coach with its four-horse team?
Its sturdy driver, — who remembers him?
Or the old landlord, saturnine and grim,
Who left our hill-top for a new abode
And reared his sign-post farther down the road?
Still in the waters of the dark Shawshine
Do the young bathers splash and think they're clean?
Do pilgrims find their way to Indian Ridge,
Or journey onward to the far-off bridge,
And bring to younger ears the story back
Of the broad stream, the mighty Merrimac?
Are there still truant feet that stray beyond
These circling bounds to Pomp's or Haggett's Pond,
Or where the legendary name recalls
The forest's earlier tenant, — " Deer-jump Falls "?

Yes, every nook these youthful feet explore,
Just as our sires and grandsires did of yore;
So all life's opening paths, where nature led
Their father's feet, the children's children tread.
Roll the round century's five score years away,
Call from our storied past that earliest day
When great Eliphalet (I can see him now, —
Big name, big frame, big voice, and beetling brow),
Then *young* Eliphalet, — ruled the rows of boys
In homespun gray or old-world corduroys, —

And save for fashion's whims, the benches show
The self-same youths, the very boys we know.
Time works strange marvels: since I trod the green
And swung the gates, what wonders I have seen !
But come what will, — the sky itself may fall —
As things of course the boy accepts them all.
The prophet's chariot, drawn by steeds of flame,
For daily use our travelling millions claim;
The face we love a sunbeam makes our own;
No more the surgeon hears the sufferer's groan;
What unwrit histories wrapped in darkness lay
Till shovelling Schliemann bared them to the day !
Your Richelieu says, and says it well, my lord,
The pen is (sometimes) mightier than the sword;
Great is the goosequill, say we all; Amen !
Sometimes the spade is mightier than the pen ;
It shows where Babel's terraced walls were raised,
The slabs that cracked when Nimrod's palace blazed,
Unearths Mycenæ, rediscovers Troy, —
Calmly he listens, that immortal boy.
A new Prometheus tips our wands with fire,
A mightier Orpheus strains the whispering wire,
Whose lightning thrills the lazy winds outrun
And hold the hours as Joshua stayed the sun, —
So swift, in truth, we hardly find a place
For those dim fictions known as time and space.
Still a new miracle each year supplies, —
See at his work the chemist of the skies,

Who questions Sirius in his tortured rays
And steals the secret of the solar blaze;
Hush! while the window-rattling bugles play
The nation's airs a hundred miles away!
That wicked phonograph! hark! how it swears!
Turn it again and make it say its prayers!
And was it true, then, what the story said
Of Oxford's friar and his brazen head?
While wandering Science stands, herself perplexed
At each day's miracle, and asks "What next?"
The immortal boy, the coming heir of all,
Springs from his desk to "urge the flying ball,"
Cleaves with his bending oar the glassy waves,
With sinewy arm the dashing current braves,
The same bright creature in these haunts of ours
That Eton shadowed with her "antique towers."

Boy! Where is he? the long-limbed youth in-
    quires,
Whom his rough chin with manly pride inspires;
Ah, when the ruddy cheek no longer glows,
When the bright hair is white as winter snows,
When the dim eye has lost its lambent flame,
Sweet to his ear will be his school-boy name!
Nor think the difference mighty as it seems
Between life's morning and its evening dreams;
Fourscore, like twenty, has its tasks and toys;
In earth's wide school-house all are girls and boys.

Brothers, forgive my wayward fancy.   Who
Can guess beforehand what his pen will do ?
Too light my strain for listeners such as these,
Whom graver thoughts and soberer speech shall
     please.
Is he not here whose breath of holy song
Has raised the downcast eyes of faith so long?
Are they not here, the strangers in your gates,
For whom the wearied ear impatient waits, —
The large-brained scholars whom their toils re-
     lease, —
The bannered heralds of the Prince of Peace ?

Such was the gentle friend whose youth unblamed
In years long past our student-benches claimed;
Whose name, illumined on the sacred page,
Lives in the labors of his riper age ;
Such he whose record time's destroying march
Leaves uneffaced on Zion's springing arch :
Not to the scanty phrase of measured song,
Cramped in its fetters, names like these belong ;
One ray they lend to gild my slender line —
Their praise I leave to sweeter lips than mine.

Home of our sires, where learning's temple rose,
While yet they struggled with their banded foes,
As in the West thy century's sun descends,
One parting gleam its dying radiance lends.

Darker and deeper though the shadows fall
From the gray towers on Doubting Castle's wall,
Though Pope and Pagan re-array their hosts,
And her new armor youthful Science boasts,
Truth, for whose altar rose this holy shrine,
Shall fly for refuge to these bowers of thine;
No past shall chain her with its rusted vow,
No Jew's phylactery bind her Christian brow,
But Faith shall smile to find her sister free,
And nobler manhood draw its life from thee.

Long as the arching skies above thee spread,
As on thy groves the dews of heaven are shed,
With currents widening still from year to year,
And deepening channels, calm, untroubled, clear,
Flow the twin streamlets from thy sacred hill —
Pieria's fount and Siloam's shaded rill!

THE SILENT MELODY.

"Bring me my broken harp," he said ;
  "We both are wrecks, — but as ye will, —
  Though all its ringing tones have fled,
    Their echoes linger round it still ;
  It had some golden strings, I know,
  But that was long, — how long ! — ago.

"I cannot see its tarnished gold,
    I cannot hear its vanished tone,
  Scarce can my trembling fingers hold
    The pillared frame so long their own ;
  We both are wrecks, — a while ago
  It had some silver strings, I know,

"But on them Time too long has played
    The solemn strain that knows no change,
  And where of old my fingers strayed
    The chords they find are new and strange, —
  Yes ! iron strings, — I know, — I know, —
  We both are wrecks of long ago.

" We both are wrecks, — a shattered pair, —
　　Strange to ourselves in time's disguise . . . .
What say ye to the lovesick air
　　That brought the tears from Marian's eyes ?
Ay ! trust me, — under breasts of snow
Hearts could be melted long ago !

" Or will ye hear the storm-song's crash
　　That from his dreams the soldier woke,
And bade him face the lightning flash
　　When battle's cloud in thunder broke ? . . . .
Wrecks, — nought but wrecks ! — the time was
　　when
We two were worth a thousand men ! "

And so the broken harp they bring
　　With pitying smiles that none could blame ;
Alas ! there 's not a single string
　　Of all that filled the tarnished frame !
But see ! like children overjoyed,
His fingers rambling through the void !

" I clasp thee ! Ay . . . . mine ancient lyre . . . .
　　Nay, guide my wandering fingers. . . . . . There !
They love to dally with the wire
　　As Isaac played with Esau's hair. . . . . .
Hush ! ye shall hear the famous tune
That Marian called the The Breath of June ! "

6

And so they softly gather round :
    Rapt in his tuneful trance he seems :
His fingers move : but not a sound !
    A silence like the song of dreams. . . . .
" There ! ye have heard the air," he cries,
" That brought the tears from Marian's eyes ! "

Ah, smile not at his fond conceit,
    Nor deem his fancy wrought in vain ;
To him the unreal sounds are sweet, —
    No discord mars the silent strain
Scored on life's latest, starlit page —
The voiceless melody of age.

Sweet are the lips of all that sing,
    When Nature's music breathes unsought,
But never yet could voice or string
    So truly shape our tenderest thought
As when by life's decaying fire
Our fingers sweep the stringless lyre !

www.ingramcontent.com/pod-product-compliance
Lightning Source LLC
Chambersburg PA
CBHW032358020726
47499CB00008B/2807